**Welcome to ALADDIN QUIX!**

If you are looking for fast, fun-to-read stories with colorful characters, lots of kid-friendly humor, easy-to-follow action, entertaining story lines, and lively illustrations, then **ALADDIN QUIX** is for you!

But wait, there's more!

If you're also looking for stories with tables of contents; word lists; about-the-book questions; 64, 80, or 96 pages; short chapters; short paragraphs; and large fonts, then **ALADDIN QUIX** is *definitely* for you!

**ALADDIN QUIX:** The next step between ready to reads and longer, more challenging chapter books, for readers five to eight years old.

Read more ALADDIN QUIX books!

*Our Principal Is a Frog!*
by Stephanie Calmenson

*Royal Sweets: A Royal Rescue*
by Helen Perelman

*A Miss Mallard Mystery: Dig to Disaster*
by Robert Quackenbush

A Miss Mallard Mystery

# TEXAS TRAIL TO CALAMITY

ROBERT QUACKENBUSH

ALADDIN QUIX

New York London Toronto Sydney New Delhi

First for Piet and all my friends in Texas,

and now for Emma and Aidan

ALADDIN QUIX
Simon & Schuster Children's Publishing Division
1230 Avenue of the Americas, New York, New York 10020
This Aladdin QUIX paperback edition May 2018

Also available in an Aladdin QUIX hardcover edition.

For information about special discounts for bulk purchases, please contact
Simon & Schuster Special Sales at 1-866-506-1949 or business@simonandschuster.com.
The Simon & Schuster Speakers Bureau can bring authors to your live event. For more information or to book an event contact the Simon & Schuster Speakers Bureau at 1-866-248-3049 or visit our website at www.simonspeakers.com.
Designed by Nina Simoneaux
The illustrations for this book were rendered in pen and ink and wash.
The text of this book was set in Archer Medium.
Manufactured in the United States of America 0418 OFF
2 4 6 8 10 9 7 5 3 1
The Library of Congress has cataloged a previous edition as follows:
Quackenbush, Robert M.
Texas trail to calamity.
Summary: When her horse runs away with her across the desert, Miss Mallard, the famous ducktective, finds herself at a forbidding ranch where she must spend the night despite mysterious warnings about her safety.
[1. Mystery and detective stories. 2. Ducks—Fiction 3. West (U.S.)—Fiction.] I. Title.
PZ7.Q16Te 1986 [Fic.] 86-4991
ISBN 978-1-5344-1310-8 (hc) • ISBN 978-1-5344-1309-2 (pbk) • ISBN 978-1-5344-1311-5 (eBook)

# Contents

# Cast of Characters

**Miss Mallard:** World-famous ducktective

**Horace and Florence Butterball:** Owners of the house Miss Mallard goes to after falling off a horse

**Cindy Butterball:** Daughter of Harold and Florence

**Phil and Tessie Dabbler:** Guests

**Mrs. Scaup:** Housekeeper for the Butterballs

**Clarence:** Cook and baker for the Butterballs

**Sheriff Teal:** Local law officer

# What's in Miss Mallard's Bag?

Miss Mallard has many detective tools she brings with her on her adventures around the world.

In her knitting bag she usually has:

- Newspaper clippings
- Knitting needles and yarn
- A magnifying glass
- A flashlight
- A mirror
- A travel guide
- Chocolates for her nephew

# 1

## Lost on the Prairie

**Miss Mallard**, the world-famous ducktective, was on vacation at a dude ranch in Texas. Late one afternoon she went horseback riding.

Out on the trail, her horse was

suddenly frightened by a bouncing **tumbleweed**.

Her horse squealed and reared up on his hind legs. Miss Mallard went crashing to the ground, knitting bag and all. Then her horse galloped back to the ranch.

She was left alone on the prairie to find her own way back.

Soon it grew dark. Miss Mallard saw some lights in the distance and headed toward them. At last she came to a huge, old house.

Miss Mallard firmly **clutched**

her knitting bag and climbed the steps of the spooky-looking house. When she rang the doorbell, a housekeeper opened the door.

"I fell off my horse," said Miss Mallard. "And I am lost. May I use your telephone?"

The housekeeper invited her inside. There Miss Mallard met the owners of the house—**Horace** and **Florence Butterball** and their daughter, **Cindy**.

With them were their guests, **Phil** and **Tessie Dabbler**. They

gathered around Miss Mallard, excited to have a famous duck-tective in their midst.

"You *must* spend the night with us," said Florence Butterball, "and let us treat you to some Texas-style **hospitality**."

"Oh, but I can't," said Miss Mallard. "I'm expected back at the Duckaroo Dude Ranch. They are probably searching for me at this very moment."

"We'll call them!" said Horace Butterball. "You must stay for our

cookout tomorrow morning and then the celebration in our beautiful city of San Antonio. We're going to make a Texan out of you!"

"It does sound wonderful!" said Miss Mallard. "But . . ."

"**Good!** Then it's settled!" said Florence Butterball.

She quickly turned to the housekeeper.

"**Mrs. Scaup,**" she said, "please call the ranch. Tell them that Miss Mallard is safe and that she will spend the night with us. Then prepare the Gold Room for her and tell **Clarence**, the cook, that we have another guest."

Mrs. Scaup said sourly, "I don't think Clarence will like the idea of an unexpected guest, Madam. It's too much work."

**"Don't be silly!"** Florence Butterball replied. "Clarence is a terrific cook. He enjoys making new dishes! He'll be thrilled when he learns that the guest is Miss Mallard, the famous ducktective."

Mrs. Scaup left in a huff. Shortly afterward she rang a bell calling everyone to come for dinner.

Horace Butterball **grumbled**, "Our new housekeeper gives me the creeps with her **snooty** ways and ringing bells and all."

"Now, dear," said his wife. "She's just being **efficient**. Haven't you noticed the house is spotless and she checks everything for dust with her white gloves?"

**"Duck waddle!"** said Horace. "Let's eat."

# 2

# Old Treasure

At dinner, the conversation was lively and interesting to Miss Mallard. Much of it was about Texas history, which she found fascinating.

There was even an unsolved

crime for Miss Mallard to **ponder**!

Many old documents and treasures from Texas's history had recently been stolen from homes all over the state. The only clues the police had were some telltale prints. But they could not identify the prints and find out who was behind the thefts.

"Here is *one* document the thieves will never get, Miss Mallard," said Horace Butterball after dinner.

"We keep it in an old leather

pouch that belonged to our first hero of early Texas, Sam Houston Drake."

Everyone gathered around a glass case in one corner of the dining room.

Horace Butterball opened the door of the glass case with a key. Then he took out the leather pouch. He opened the pouch and removed an old, torn **parchment.**

"**Come close!** This is one of the most treasured documents in all Texas," he said. "I am giving it to the State of Texas tomorrow at the Alamo National Monument in San Antonio. It is a list of the first three hundred duck families who settled in Texas, and it includes our family name."

**"Phooey!"** said Phil Dabbler to his wife, Tessie. "Our family name isn't on it. What's the big deal?"

**"I hate that list!"** snapped Tessie.

Horace was so eager to tell Miss Mallard about the list that he

forgot how the Dabblers felt about it. They were angry and **offended** about not being included, and they acted as if they thought it was Horace's fault.

Horace didn't know how to make them feel better. Quickly, he returned the document to its pouch, placed the pouch back in the case, and locked the glass door.

Everyone left the room.

"Well," he said, hoping to change the subject, "shall we go

into the library and look at some home movies?"

While the movies were being shown, the Dabblers sat **glum** and silent. But they were not the only ones who felt angry. Cindy Butterball did too. That was because the movies were about *her*.

"Oh, Daddy, do you have to?" she protested every time another film began.

Finally, after the tenth movie starring Cindy as a duckling,

Florence Butterball said, "I think it's time for us to go to bed. The celebration breakfast will be at eight in the morning in the back-yard. Then we must be at the Alamo by noon."

With that, everyone said good night.

# 3

# Mysterious Notes

Mrs. Scaup took Miss Mallard upstairs to her room. They came to a long hallway with bedroom doors on each side.

"The door to your bedroom is at the end of the hall," said

Mrs. Scaup. "Next to the door to your bedroom is the door to the back stairs. The stairs lead to the backyard, where the cookout will be in the morning."

She opened the door to Miss Mallard's bedroom and they went inside.

The room was very large and grand. In it was a four-poster bed with a warm quilt and fluffy pillows. A fancy dresser had a gold mirror hanging above it.

"Just pull the cord by the bed

if you need anything," said Mrs. Scaup.

"Thank you," said Miss Mallard.

She was about to set her knitting bag on a chair, but it **toppled** over and went tumbling to the floor. Mrs. Scaup stooped down to help pick up the things that spilled out.

**"Do be careful!"** said Miss Mallard. "I have some sticky chocolates in there somewhere. I wouldn't want you to soil your gloves on them."

Mrs. Scaup quickly removed her gloves and picked up the chocolates, a small mirror, and some news items from Miss Mallard's clipping file. When everything was back in the bag, she put on her gloves and left.

Miss Mallard got ready for bed. She put on a nightgown that Mrs. Scaup placed on the bed for her.

Then she crawled under the covers. She was very tired from her **ordeal** on the prairie.

She fell sound asleep.

Later that night, she was awakened by a noise. She opened her eyes and saw a note being slipped under her door.

She ran to the door and opened it. She looked up and down the hall, but saw no one. She picked up the note and closed the door. By her bedside lamp she read:

> Do not eat the breakfast rolls.
> From someone who cares.

Miss Mallard shivered. What did the note mean?

Miss Mallard had trouble getting back to sleep. When at last she did, she was awakened again. Another note was being slipped under her door! This note said:

Do not drink the juice at breakfast.
From someone who cares.

Miss Mallard was wide awake after the second note. She tossed and turned in her bed the rest of the night.

When dawn came, she drifted off to sleep from **exhaustion**.

Later that morning, she was awakened by sounds coming through her window from the backyard. She sat up in her bed and listened. It was the cookout!

**"Oh dear!"** she said. "I must hurry." She bolted out of bed.

In a flash, she dressed and raced down the back stairs to the yard. She expected to discover that something terrible had happened before she had a chance to warn everyone about the notes.

All because she overslept!

# 4

## At the Cookout

Outside in the backyard, everyone was gathered around a table. Clarence, the cook, was flipping pancakes on an outdoor grill. Waiters were heaping the table with great mounds of food.

Mrs. Scaup stood close by to see that everything was done properly.

Miss Mallard looked at everyone at the table.

But she didn't see any rolls or juice! **Oh no!** Had they already been eaten?

Horace Butterball was the first to see her.

"You're here, Miss Mallard!" he said. "We figured you needed your rest after being lost on the prairie yesterday, so we didn't wake you.

But there is still plenty of food. Except we quickly gobbled down the juice and rolls, I'm sorry to say."

Florence Butterball said, "But we have lots of Texas-style iced tea, and you must try some of Clarence's delicious pancakes."

Mrs. Scaup stepped forward and said, "Yes, do sit down at the table, Miss Mallard. I'll bring you some iced tea and pancakes."

Miss Mallard looked at the guests. It certainly appeared that no harm had come to anyone from

drinking the juice or eating the rolls. **What a relief!**

But she still wondered why the notes had been slipped under her door. Had anyone else received them? If she said something, would she cause a panic?

Most of all, she wondered who did it. She thought about the second note.

Then she remembered that it had a grease spot on it. It was the only clue she had until she could compare the handwriting on the notes with the handwriting of everyone in the house. But that was impossible to do during the cookout.

There was nothing she could do but wait.

All through breakfast Miss Mallard picked at the pancakes with her fork. She felt too uneasy to eat or drink anything. It was the longest meal of her life.

At last it was over. Miss Mallard heaved a sigh of relief. Nothing terrible had happened to her or anyone at the table.

"Cindy," said Horace Butterball. "Please get the leather pouch from the glass case in the dining room. Here is the key. We'll have a toast to our ancestors to finish our feast. Then we'll be on our way to deliver the document to the state museum at the Alamo."

Cindy went into the house, but she was back in a flash.

**"Daddy!"** she cried. "The glass case! Someone broke into it!"

# 5

## Scene of the Crime

Everyone ran to the dining room and gathered around the glass case. They saw that the door to the case was broken.

**"What happened?"** cried Cindy.

On the floor was the leather pouch. But the flap of the pouch was open.

The document inside was gone!

Tessie Dabbler gasped.

**"Step aside! Everyone, step aside!"** said Miss Mallard. "Please don't touch anything."

"I'll call **Sheriff Teal** to come at once," said Horace Butterball. He rushed out of the room.

"In the meantime, I'll check the glass case for prints," said Miss Mallard.

Taking a magnifying glass from her knitting bag, she **examined** the case. Miss Mallard saw many different prints.

Then she remembered how everyone had gathered around the case after dinner. "They must have left their prints on the glass then," she thought.

Soon Sheriff Teal arrived with his **deputies.**

His deputies waited outside while he examined the prints on the glass case.

The sheriff then compared them with a copy of some prints that he had brought with him.

"None of the prints on this glass case match the prints we found at one of the other robberies," he said. "Whoever stole your document is not the robber we've been hunting for."

Everyone in the room was shocked.

"**What?!** You mean one of *us* could have stolen the document?" asked Florence Butterball.

"One—or all of you," said Sheriff Teal. "The prints tell the story. All of you have touched the case at one time or another. So it would be impossible to pin the robbery on any one of you."

He started to leave.

**"Wait, Sheriff!"** said Miss Mallard. "May I have a copy of the prints that belong to the crook who **committed** the other robberies?"

Sheriff Teal handed Miss Mallard a copy of the robber's prints, and headed for the door.

"But, Sheriff!" pleaded Horace Butterball. "How can you leave like this? A treasured document has been stolen. What can I tell the crowd at the Alamo?"

"That's up to you," said Sheriff Teal. "I have no case here. All I can do is file a report and hope something turns up. Goodbye."

# 6

# Telltale Prints

As Sheriff Teal was going out the door, the Dabblers announced that they were going home.

**"You can't leave now!"** Horace Butterball said to the

Dabblers. "You must help us find that document!"

**"Phooey!"** said Phil Dabbler. "Who cares about that!"

A big argument started between the two. While they hollered at each other, Florence Butterball started **quarreling** with Clarence, the cook.

"After all," she shouted, "you were up all night preparing the breakfast! You should have been listening for robbers!"

"I didn't know I was hired to

cook for this place and guard it too," snapped Clarence.

Meanwhile Tessie Dabbler started a quarrel with Cindy, and Mrs. Scaup yelled at one of the waiters, who yelled back.

The quarreling got noisier and noisier. Finally, Miss Mallard stood on a chair and quacked as loudly as she could:

**"QUIET!"**

The room was suddenly silent.

**"There!"** said Miss Mallard. "If you will all stay quiet for a moment, I'll tell you what happened to the document. First, we must bring back the sheriff and his deputies before they drive away. Clarence! Get Sheriff Teal!"

When Sheriff Teal returned, he asked, "What is this all about?"

Miss Mallard responded, "You left before I could reveal some important information to you. Then things got a bit out of hand."

"What information?" asked Sheriff Teal.

"The identity of the thief who stole the historical treasures, including the one in this house," said Miss Mallard.

She took the small mirror from her knitting bag. There were prints on it.

Everyone crowded around the ducktective and the sheriff. They all wanted a closer look at the evidence.

She held the mirror next to the

copy of the robber's prints that the sheriff had given her. They were the same!

"I got the prints when I dropped my knitting bag," said Miss Mallard coolly. "The prints on the mirror were made with chocolate. They belong to . . ."

Before Miss Mallard could finish, Mrs. Scaup started to run.

# 7

# The Arrest

**"Stop her!"** shouted Miss Mallard.

Sheriff Teal blocked Mrs. Scaup from leaving. The treasured document fell out of a pocket of her dress.

**"You're under arrest!"** said Sheriff Teal.

He called for his deputies to take her to jail. As the deputies were leaving with Mrs. Scaup, she turned and glared at Miss Mallard.

She yelled, "I should have never let you in the house. That was my undoing!"

Then she broke out with loud, angry quacks. She was heard still quacking like that when the deputies drove her away.

"I suspected Mrs. Scaup as soon

as I saw her white gloves," said Miss Mallard. "She pretended to be a housekeeper so she could steal and sell historical treasures and documents. She wore gloves so she wouldn't leave prints at the scenes of her crimes."

She continued. "During a past crime, she must have removed her gloves, like she did for me. That was how the police got a copy of her prints. Her gloves were the reason why her prints were not on the glass case with all the others.

And that's how I knew that she had stolen the document."

"We owe you a big thanks, Miss Mallard," said Horace Butterball. "But how will we get to the Alamo in time to present the document?"

"I'll lead the way with my siren," said Sheriff Teal. **"Let's go!"**

They raced after the sheriff's car to the Alamo. When Horace Butterball took his place on the platform in front of a huge crowd, Miss Mallard turned to Clarence, the cook.

"Why did you put the notes under my door last night?" asked Miss Mallard.

Clarence blushed and said, "I wanted everything to be perfect for your first Texas cookout. The rolls I was baking last night didn't turn out right. The oranges for the juice weren't as good as usual."

"I thought that might be it," said Miss Mallard. "The clue was the grease stain I saw on the second note. I checked a news clipping about grease stains in my knitting bag. It was a butter stain. That's when I knew that the notes came from the kitchen and were your doing. Thank you for thinking of me."

**"My pleasure!"** said Clarence.

He handed Miss Mallard a box with a ribbon tied around it.

"I fixed this for you," he said. "I noticed that you didn't eat anything at the cookout. The juice and the rolls inside are perfect this time."

"How kind of you!" said Miss Mallard.

Just then Horace Butterball stood up. He began reading the names of the first three hundred Texas families.

Everyone cheered as each name was read. Then Horace came to the *M*'s.

**"WYATT MALLARD!"** he shouted.

**"Goodness!"** said Miss Mallard. "That's *my* ancestor. I guess that makes me a Texan."

# Word List

**clutched (CLUTCHED):** Grabbed tightly; held something tightly

**committed (co·MIT·ted):** Gave time and effort to an activity or event

**deputies (DEH·pew·tees):** Assistants to a person in charge of an organization

**efficient (ee·FIH·shent):** Completing an action without wasting time

**examined (ex·ZAM·ind):** Looked at closely and carefully

**exhaustion (ex·ZAWS·chun):** Being extremely tired

**glum (GLUM):** Depressed or sad

**grumbled (GRUM·buld):** Complained quietly in an unhappy way

**hospitality (HA·spi·TAH·li·tee):** Friendly treatment of visitors

**offended (uh·FEND·ed):** Caused to be angry or insulted

**ordeal (or·DEAL):** A difficult experience

**parchment (PARCH·muhnt):** Ancient paper

**ponder (PON·der):** Think about

**quarreling (KWAR·uh·ling):** Having an argument

**snooty (SNOO·tee):** An attitude of thinking you are better than another person

**toppled (TAH·pulled):** Fell over

**tumbleweed (TUM·bul·WEED):** A desert plant that breaks off near the ground and is blown around by the wind

# Questions

1. Why were the Dabblers upset with Harold Butterball?
2. Would you have been mad at him?
3. What time did the guests have to be at the Alamo?
4. Who else did you think took the document from the Butterballs' glass case?
5. What was in Miss Mallard's bag that helped her solve the mystery?

# Acknowledgments

My deepest thanks and appreciation go to Jon Anderson, president and publisher of Simon & Schuster Children's Books, and his talented team: Karen Nagel, editor; Karin Paprocki, art director; Nina Simoneaux, designer; Katherine Devendorf, managing editor; Bernadette Flinn, production manager; Tricia Lin, editorial assistant; and Richard Ackoon, executive coordinator;

for launching these incredible editions of my Miss Mallard Mystery books for today's young readers.